DISNEP

BEVERLY HILLS CHIHUAHUA

Adapted by Kate Egan

Based on the screenplay by Analisa LaBianco and Jeff Bushell
and the story by Jeff Bushell

DISNEP
PRESS

New York

Printed in the United States of America

First Edition
1 3 5 7 9 10 8 6 4 2

Library of Congress Catalog Card Number on file.
ISBN 978-1-4231-1409-3

For more Disney Press fun, visit www.disneybooks.com
Visit Disney.com/beverlyhillschihuahua

CHAPTER ONE

A Rolls-Royce turned onto Rodeo Drive in Beverly Hills, gleaming in the bright sun. It sailed past exclusive restaurants, expensive stores, and gawking tourists. All eyes were fixed on the fabulous car as it pulled up in front of Rain Spa. A beautiful woman climbed out and sashayed into the cool haven of the spa, carrying a brand-new Louis Vuitton bag. It was the one and only Vivian Ashe, a fixture on the list of who's who in Beverly Hills.

Murmurs spread through the spa as Vivian

1

made her entrance. "Oh, look, here she comes," said one of the spa's patrons, her eyes bulging. "Is that the new Louis Vuitton?"

"I might have known she'd be the first to have one," another patron said, letting out an envious sigh.

Unaware of the comments, Vivian walked past the rows of hair dryers and manicure tables straight to the back room. She set her purse down on a table—and out stepped a beautiful Chihuahua!

"Sorry I'm late!" said the dog, whose name was Chloe Winthrop Ashe. She nodded toward the purse. "We had to do a little shopping!" The two patrons who had noted her arrival trotted over and wagged their tails in greeting. This was no ordinary spa. It was a spa that catered to the pampered pooches of Beverly Hills. For them, the back room of Rain Spa was *the* place to be. And no other pet was quite as pampered as Vivian's Chihuahua, Chloe. Vivian took

Chloe everywhere and bought her the best of everything. Other dogs were green with envy.

"I'm so jealous," said one of the regulars, a chocolate toy poodle named Delta. She was eyeing Chloe's bag. "Do you love it?"

Chloe grinned. "I'm practically living in it!" she joked.

Liberace, a pug with attitude, trotted up to Chloe. His eyes were fixed on her neck. "Tell me the stones in that collar are not real!" he said in disbelief.

Chloe turned her head to show it off. "Van Cleef & Arpels. Viv said I *had* to have it!"

Vivian couldn't understand dog language. To people, their chatter just sounded like barking. And so it was unintentional that Vivian interrupted the doggie conversation. "A brush and seaweed wrap, Armand, and I need to pick her up at noon," Vivian said briskly. "We're having lunch with my niece at the Four Seasons." She bent down and kissed Chloe's head. "Ciao, darling," she murmured.

"She's so good to me," Chloe told the other dogs as Vivian left the store. Life was good for a lapdog in Beverly Hills—especially Vivian Ashe's lapdog.

By the time noon rolled around, Chloe's fur was shining and she'd caught up on all the gossip with her friends. Vivian reappeared and whisked Chloe away. Then it was back to the stores! Perched in Viv's purse, Chloe rode jauntily from boutique to boutique while Viv worked her cell phone to plan the upcoming European launch of her new cruelty-free skin-care line.

Chloe half-listened while a saleswoman helped her try on outfits. Would she be getting the chartreuse twin set with the matching booties today? Or the black, sequined top? Chloe settled on a pink Chanel jacket just in time to head to lunch. She was feeling great in her new outfit, and the Four Seasons was Chloe's favorite restaurant when she couldn't eat in Paris.

Only a short while later, perched on her booster seat, Chloe listened as the waiter described her choices. "Today we have seared diver scallops with crème fraiche and caviar. Swordfish on baby greens. And prawns with a tomato chutney."

Chloe sniffed each plate and tapped the scallops with her paw. "Ah, of course, the usual, Miss Chloe," the waiter said with a bow. As quickly as possible, he returned with the order, placed it in front of her, and filled her bowl with Evian. When he was done, Viv waved her hand in the air. "Go ahead and start, Chloe. I'll wait for Rachel."

The dog's tiny mouth was watering. But just as Chloe was about to take her first dainty bite, twenty-four-year-old Rachel Ashe barreled through the restaurant with her usual lack of style. "Sorry I'm late, Aunt Viv!" Rachel practically shouted. She dived for the nearest chair—which just happened to be where Chloe was sitting.

5

Rachel heard Chloe yip a second before she squashed her. Chloe waited for her to apologize, but all Rachel said was, "Oh, Chloe, I didn't see you."

"I'll bet," Chloe muttered to herself. "I thought something that big was supposed to beep when it backed up."

Viv's niece settled into another chair and grabbed Chloe's plate. "I'm starving," she announced. "Is this caviar?"

"That's *Chloe's*," Viv said firmly.

Rachel pushed the plate back and eyed her aunt. "You know, you totally spoil this dog," she said.

"It makes me happy, darling. What can I say?" Viv replied, stroking Chloe's head, then quickly changing the subject. "Now, how are you, Rachel? How have things been going at your job?"

It didn't surprise Chloe when Rachel told her aunt she'd been fired—for the *fourth* time.

"I just don't seem to fit in anywhere," Rachel complained.

Well, you certainly don't fit in here, either, Chloe thought. *And you won't until you learn to appreciate the finer things in life.*

Viv was more sympathetic. She told Rachel about the risks she took when she was young. People saw her potential and gave her a chance. And it had all been worth it.

"I wish somebody would see me that way," said Rachel wistfully.

Her aunt patted her hand. "It doesn't matter how other people see you, Rachel. What matters is how you see yourself."

Chloe rolled her eyes. She knew Viv's advice came from the heart, but Rachel wouldn't listen. She never did.

Back at Viv's estate after lunch, Chloe settled in by the pool in her favorite polka-dot bikini. She stretched out in her pint-size chaise and adjusted her sunglasses.

It was time to get some sun.

In one of the home's surrounding land-scaped gardens, Viv was talking to Sam Cortez, the landscaper, about a new project—Viv loved planning additions to her beautiful grounds. Chloe had no problems with Sam. But his dog, Papi, was another story. He was always getting underfoot and saying the most inappropriate things.

Her eyes still closed, Chloe felt a shadow fall on her. "You're blocking my sun," she growled.

Ignoring Chloe's tone, Papi serenaded her with a little song. "*Mi corazon*, you shine so much brighter than the sun. Why won't you be my one?"

Chloe tried not to laugh. Papi was a Chihuahua, too, but that was about all they had in common. His paws were rough from working in the garden. His fur was dirty and snarled—he'd probably never even heard of conditioner. Chloe supposed he was nice enough, but he wasn't someone she would ever socialize with.

Chloe smiled, a little flattered despite herself. Then she sat up and sniffed. "What's that smell?"

"Which one?" asked Papi. "The sweat of my labor or the mint patch I rolled in for you?"

"Neither," Chloe trailed off. It was something else. And it wasn't good.

"Then it must be the fertilizer," Papi said.

Chloe knew what that meant. Manure! "Gross!" she yelled, shrinking away from him. "You're covered in it!"

"Of course!" bragged Papi. "I am a landscaper. He nudged something toward Chloe with his paw. "Grasshopper, *mi corazon*? I caught it myself. Very tasty."

"Papi, that's disgusting," squealed Chloe. As *if* she would ever dream of eating an insect!

But Papi never gave up. "I will leave it here in case you change your mind."

Chloe was saved by the ringing of the mansion's doorbell. She rose haughtily and brushed Papi off, saying "Excuse me, we have guests."

Papi watched through the glass doors as Chloe greeted Vivian's niece. Just then, Sam appeared beside Papi and looked in the same direction. "Careful, amigo," Sam cautioned. "You don't want that kind of trouble." Sam led his dog away, but not before Papi noticed him stealing his own glance—at Rachel.

CHAPTER TWO

"Don't yip at me, Chloe," Rachel ordered as she entered the foyer. "Where's Aunt Viv? Go find Aunt Viv. Find her, girl."

Chloe stood her ground, refusing to budge. "Who am I?" she grumbled. "Lassie?"

"You're so completely useless," Rachel snapped.

Just then, Viv walked into the entryway, talking on the phone. "No, of course I understand," she said, sounding upset. She glanced distractedly at Rachel and waved her closer. "No, really, it's wonderful news. Don't worry about a thing. Enjoy this time with your family."

Viv was totally frazzled when she hung up. Chloe bounded over to give her a kiss, but Rachel got to her first. "Are you okay, Aunt Viv?" she asked with concern.

"Oh, Rachel, I'm so sorry," Viv replied, "I'm not going to be able to have brunch today. I'm on a plane this afternoon, the staff is off, and Chloe's nanny had her baby six weeks early."

"You're not taking Chloe with you?" Rachel asked, shocked that her aunt would leave the dog home.

Viv looked taken aback. "On vacation, sure—but this is business. And four cities in ten days. She's much too delicate for that kind of travel."

"What about a kennel?" Rachel asked brightly.

Over my dead body, thought Chloe. Viv

picked the dog up and petted her, as if to reassure her.

"No, no, no," Viv said. "I could never leave Chloe in the hands of *strangers*." She fell silent for a moment, caressing Chloe's head and staring out the window at her magnificent gardens. Suddenly, she looked at Rachel. "But *you're* not a stranger, Rachel. . . ."

Next thing Chloe knew, Viv was giving her a good-bye kiss and handing her over to Rachel—of all people! A limo waited in the driveway. Chloe clung to Viv for as long as she could, brightening only when Viv reminded Rachel, "I'm entrusting you with my greatest treasure." Choking back tears, Chloe watched the limo disappear into the hills. She just knew her time with Rachel was going to be a nightmare.

Chloe had places to go and dogs to see, and Rachel didn't seem to understand. When Chloe's friends showed up with their nannies, for their usual pool time, Rachel raised an eyebrow and asked "A playdate?" as if it were the most ridiculous thing she'd ever heard.

While Chloe lay on her chaise, too depressed to do anything else, Rachel sat on the other side of the pool, gossiping with two of her friends about Chloe! "Don't get me started on her schedule," Rachel whispered not-so-softly to her friends Angela and Blair. "Shiatsu massages, couture fittings, doggie birthday parties . . . it's insane!" Rachel really knew how to hurt a dog's feelings.

Chloe's friends, Bimini, Delta, and Liberace, gathered near her and tried to be supportive. But Chloe was distracted by the bizarre sight of Papi jumping up and down behind a hedge as he tried to get a peek at them. *Now you see him . . . now you don't*, thought Chloe. *Now you see him . . . now you don't.*

"Who is that hunky Chihuahua over there?" asked Delta.

"The gardener," Chloe said. She wasn't

in the mood for this. Couldn't Papi just go away?

But he didn't go away. Instead, he chose this moment to try to make some kind of big impression. "Excuse me while I bravely defend your garden from that dangerous bird," he announced with a flourish. The next thing Chloe knew, Papi was bounding after a perfectly ordinary sparrow, leaping over Rachel and her friends like a track star over hurdles.

Papi caught the small bird in his teeth and gave it, still squirming, to Chloe. "*Perdoname por favor*, but my heart must speak. I only wish to say that if you ever need someone to lick inside your ears, or chew the hard-to-reach places, or share your slumber in the sun, I would be most honored to be that special someone."

Just when she wished she would sink into the ground and away from the shocked looks of her friends, Sam called Papi off.

"That is one hot dog," said Bimini, as Papi bounded away.

"But we're from two different worlds," Chloe reminded her. "I could never be with a dog who's proud of being from the pound." She had standards, after all!

The next morning, Chloe nipped at Rachel's elbow, trying to wake her up. "Come on," Chloe urged. "I've got a mani-pedi at eleven." Chloe couldn't miss her weekly appointment! But her barking didn't seem to register. The only thing that roused Rachel was the sound of a rumbling backhoe in the garden. Apparently, Sam was about to start working on Vivian's new koi pond. Papi was by his side.

Chloe watched Rachel storm off and try to reason with Sam. It was obviously too early for him to be doing noisy construction. He didn't seem to understand her, though—and it was hard to take her seriously when she was still in her pajamas and trying to use

gestures to get her point across. Rachel stomped back into the house, ignored Chloe's yipping, and picked up the ringing phone.

"Hello? Angela?!" Rachel shouted. "No, don't bother coming over! Whatshisname's digging some big hole! I tried to stop him, but he doesn't speak English. What?" Rachel listened for a moment, then squealed. "You're a genius! Give me thirty minutes!"

For the first time since she'd arrived, Rachel smiled at Chloe. "Pack your bikini, Chloe," she cried. "We're going on a trip!"

A short while later, Chloe found herself sitting next to Rachel in the back of Angela's BMW convertible, the wind ruffling her fur. Rachel's friends sat in the backseat. She didn't mind so much that her blow-out was getting ruined—it was nice to get out of the house. But her heart sank when the car approached the crowded Tijuana border crossing. All Chloe could see, beneath a big sign for Mexico, was a long line of cars and buses clogging the road ahead of her. The smell of their exhaust mixed with the smell of sausage cooking by the side of the road. This wasn't the kind of place Viv would want her to be, to say the least.

After driving for what felt like hours, Angela pulled into a shabby beach town that seemed to be stuck in the last century. Bleached adobe houses crowded a main square, their red-tile roofs baking in the sun. Children splashed in a central fountain, and older people chatted near a line of colorful taco stands. Bright flowers grew everywhere, and the ocean glinted behind the square, promising sand and surf for throngs of tourists. But Chloe wasn't one to appreciate the town's laid-back charm. And everywhere she looked she saw bony dogs begging for food. Chloe was disgusted.

Angela checked everyone into what she called a "hotel" and then led the way upstairs to their room. She turned a bent metal key in the lock, and the door squeaked open. Chloe couldn't believe her eyes. Was that a hole in the carpet? And where was the Jacuzzi? Yes, the view of the water was nice, but Chloe had seen the ocean before. "This isn't the Four Seasons," she grumbled. "This isn't even *one* season."

But Rachel was obviously pleased and excited. She threw Chloe into her beach bag with some towels and a bottle of sunscreen, then headed for the shore. Chloe had barely poked her head out of the tote before Rachel and her friends were running toward a pair of surfers they seemed to know from home. "Hey, guys," one of the boys said to Rachel and her friends. "We didn't know you were coming down here."

"It was an emergency evacuation," Rachel joked.

One of the boys noticed Chloe inside the beach bag and stopped to pet her. "What a cutie," he said.

Rachel cooed. "Yeah, isn't she? I'm taking care of her while my aunt's in Europe."

Hmph, thought Chloe. Apparently being near cute boys was the only way she was going to get some decent treatment from Rachel.

Chloe tried to nap in the bag while the girls flirted with the surfers, but who could sleep with all that giggling? That night, she miserably watched the sun set while the girls got ready to go out to some club.

Rachel disappeared into the hotel bathroom and came out a few moments later with a Frisbee full of stinking dog food. "Dinnertime," she chirped. It was all Chloe could do to keep from gagging. When no one was looking, Chloe picked up a chunk of the nasty glop and dropped it in Rachel's shoe. What had Rachel expected her to do with that stuff? Chloe certainly wasn't going to eat it!

The girls looked like they were about to

head out to dinner, so Chloe leaped back into Rachel's bag. Finally, I'll get some real food, she thought with relief.

Rachel's friend Blair spotted Chloe in the bag and came over to stroke her ears. "She's so cute," she said. "Why don't we take her with us?"

Rachel shook her head. "I am *not* taking a dog dancing," she said, narrowing her eyes at Chloe. "You're not even a real dog. You're an accessory. And tonight you don't go with my outfit." With that, Rachel yanked Chloe out of her bag and ushered her friends out of the room.

It was the last straw. Chloe was starving, filthy, and about to be left alone in a fleabag hotel. She ran out onto the balcony and yipped at the girls as they walked away and into the night. "Come back here!" In her anger, she knocked against a flowerpot and pushed it off the balcony. She watched as it plummeted through the air and smashed on the ground below. "Oops," said Chloe to no one in particular. "Just add that to the bill."

A short time later, a doorman came from downstairs to investigate. Chloe realized that this was her opportunity. After knocking on the door the doorman opened it cautiously. In a flash, Chloe slipped between his legs and into the elevator! Free at last!

She strutted into the lobby and marched past a surprised desk clerk, her head held high. She would not put up with being locked up for another second. Chloe was going to find Rachel and show her that she was a dog to be reckoned with.

Once she was out on the street, Chloe heard the strains of salsa music and saw the flames of bonfires coming from the beach in the distance. She wandered through a maze of streets crowded with partyers, neon signs were blazing in the windows of bars and nightclubs.

Finally, just ahead, she spotted Rachel and

her friends. They were about to enter a club. After the chaos of the streets, Chloe was almost happy to see Rachel. "There you are!" she cried as she trotted to catch up with the girls.

Chloe stepped carefully off a curb and into the street. But before she got any farther, a tall man with a sinister face loomed above her. As Rachel sauntered into the club without a care in the world, the leering man grabbed Chloe and stuffed her into a van!

CHAPTER THREE

"Rachel, help me!" cried Chloe as the van door slammed. "Somebody, please! I'm being dognapped! Help!" But nobody could hear her through the thick doors of the van or above the incessant beat of the music in the street.

Chloe was surrounded by darkness, but she could hear a rustling sound coming from somewhere in the van. She shrank away from the noise just as a streetlight revealed the faces of several frightened dogs cowering in the corner.

"*A donde nos llevan, senorita?*" a terrified voice whispered.

The dog was speaking Spanish and Chloe didn't understand a word. "I don't understand you," Chloe said slowly and loudly. "Where are they taking us?" But it was no good. All the other dogs did was shake their heads and whimper as the tall man drove the van ever deeper into Mexico.

Much later that night, Rachel arrived back at the hotel, glowing. She couldn't remember the last time she'd had so much fun. She tossed her purse on the bed and looked around. The room seemed empty.

"Chloe? Chloe, come out. I'm not in the mood." Rachel checked the bathroom and under the beds, but she couldn't find her aunt's dog anywhere. "I mean it. Stop hiding. I'm sorry I gave you dog food. I'll order you room service for breakfast." But there was still no response.

After a while, Rachel gave up looking and went to bed. But nagging guilt kept her from sleeping much that night. In the morning, she looked all over and finally headed for the local animal shelter. "I searched the beach, the boardwalk," she explained to the shelter's director. "I put up signs at the hotel. . . . I'm just praying she's here."

Rachel's heart sank as she walked past rows of caged dogs, their wet noses pressed against the bars. There were dogs of every breed and every shape and size . . . but none of them was Chloe.

"Where could she be?" Rachel sighed, stumped. "She barely walks anywhere, let alone runs."

A grim expression fell over the shelter director's face. "Well . . ." she began.

"What is it?" asked Rachel quickly.

"*Las peleas de perros* were in town," the

director continued. Meeting Rachel's blank stare, she added, "Dogfights."

"What does that have to do with Chloe?"

The shelter director spelled it out. "When they come through, dogs always disappear. They put them in the ring to fight. Or, worse, to use as bait."

Rachel took a deep breath. "How can I find them?"

The shelter director stared at the floor and tried to break the bad news gently. "They're criminals, so they're always on the move. Rumor is their next stop is Mexico City."

In an industrial area of Mexico City, dim lights shone from behind the barred windows of a domed warehouse. Inside, a seedy crowd sat in makeshift bleachers surrounding a caged ring. Bets were being placed on two dogs who would soon be forced to face off against each other.

Downstairs, the van driver who'd taken

Chloe was playing solitaire. Behind him, dogs paced nervously in dingy wooden corrals.

Chloe trembled in the corner of her dark enclosure. "Where am I?" she asked, but no one answered. All she knew was that she was a long, long way from Beverly Hills. A German shepherd in the next corral poked his nose around the wall between them. "You're in the dogfights."

He was cut short by a voice coming from a walkie-talkie. "Next bout's in two."

Chloe took in her surroundings for a minute. She noticed the loser from the last fight slinking in, defeated. Then she shook her head slowly. This all had to be a terrible mistake. "This is outrageous," she yipped. "I was born to shop, not fight. Unless it's at a sales rack."

The German shepherd interrupted her lament. "Quit whining, *Princesa*," he said wearily. "It doesn't help."

The nerve! thought Chloe. "Chloe Winthrop

Ashe does not whine," she informed him, sticking her chin in the air.

He didn't bother to respond. But a nervous terrier named Rafa did. "You won't get any sympathy from Delgado, *senorita*. He's a gladiator," she said. "You know, a fighter. Delgado's the best of the best."

Milagros, a grouchy pit bull, broke in. "Don't listen to her, *chica*. *El Diablo's* the meanest dog in the fights. Word is, they fought once and Delgado didn't come out on top."

Whatever, thought Chloe. She wasn't taking sides in this argument. Her eyes wandered over to another dog murmuring in Spanish. "What's he saying?" she asked the pit bull.

"He always prays before a fight," Milagros said. "Don't you speak any Spanish, *chica*?"

"The name's Chloe, not *chica*," Chloe snapped. "And why would I speak Spanish?"

The pit bull's eyes grew wide as he looked Chloe over. "You're a Chihuahua, that's why!"

Chloe dimly remembered that Chihuahuas

were originally from Mexico. But she wasn't very in touch with her roots. "So?" she replied. "I'm from Beverly Hills. You know, 9-0-2-1-0? And I'm an heiress!"

Delgado, the German shepherd, seemed annoyed by the chattering. He growled. "Look, if you're worth something, they ransom you. And if they ransom you, they won't fight you. So you got nothing to worry about."

That's a relief, thought Chloe. She couldn't wait for Viv to find out what Rachel had done and for everything to get straightened out. She brushed some dirt from the corner, then settled in on the cold floor to wait.

Just as she considered closing her eyes for a catnap, a pair of hands grabbed her. "Well," Chloe said haughtily, "it's about time that you upgraded my accommodations."

On her way out of the holding corrals, Chloe could hear an announcer introducing the first dog in the next fight. "When he catches your scent, he won't stop until he smells blood! Weighing in at one hundred and eighty bone-crushing pounds. You know him, you love him. *El campeon . . . Ellll Diablo!*" It was the dog Milagros said had beaten Delgado. The crowd went wild. Beyond the cheering audience, Chloe caught a quick glimpse of El Diablo. He was a muscle-bound Doberman, and his handlers could barely control him.

Chloe was still being carried down the hall when the next dog was introduced. "And now the challenger," the announcer continued. "That *casta noble* who stood at the side of Aztec kings. Legendary warriors and mighty protectors. Weighing in at a whopping six pounds. She's lean, she's mean, and she looks good in pink. I give you . . . Chi-chi-WOW-ha!"

Next thing Chloe knew, she was being pushed into the ring! The lights were blinding and the applause was deafening. But if there was one thing Chloe loved, it was attention. "Thank you, thank you," she cried, looking around at the audience. "You're too kind. Really. This is so much nicer than that stinky corral. . . ."

It was only then that she noticed the Doberman coming toward her. His shoulders were hunched and his head was down. His pointy ears poked up like a devil's horns. *Uh-oh*, thought Chloe. Suddenly she realized what was going on. She was supposed to *fight* him!

"Oh . . . I'm sorry . . . I thought I was alone, Mr. El Diablo," she stammered nervously. "Well . . . it's certainly nice to meet you. But, you know, I really have to be going—" As she babbled, she backed away . . . until El Diablo smashed his giant paw down, just barely missing Chloe's head!

"Not so fast," he snarled. "People like a show." The audience cheered wildly, and El Diablo bared his teeth at Chloe.

"You know, I've got a dentist who could do something about that yellowing," she went on. "I mean, I get the idea that teeth are important in your line of work." El Diablo snapped, and Chloe leaped into the air. How was she going to get out of *this*?

The van driver was watching the fight with a steely-eyed, well-dressed businessman named Vasquez. "Whose idea was this, Rafferty?" the well-dressed man demanded.

"Uh, mine, Senor Vasquez," the driver admitted. He'd had this match up in mind ever since he picked up that Chihuahua back near the border. It had never occurred to him that his boss wouldn't enjoy it.

Vasquez watched El Diablo toying with Chloe in the ring. "Not bad," he sighed. "But you'd better grab another mutt. El Diablo's getting bored."

Relieved, Rafferty headed back downstairs. This he could fix.

CHAPTER FOUR

Back in the corrals, the other dogs were listening to the fight. They could hear El Diablo's fierce growling and Chloe's pitiful cries of fear. "Dog that size, there won't be much left of her," Milagros said, shaking his head.

Delgado was pacing back and forth in his corral. He was used to the sounds of fighting, but this was different. It was a total mismatch, bound to be a bloodbath, and he couldn't just stand by and listen to the little Chihuahua get torn apart. With his paw, he deftly batted at the pin that kept his cage door shut.

Watching his door swing open, one of the other dogs said "Hey, how'd you do that?" Delgado didn't stop to answer—the others would have to figure it out on their own.

He bounded up the stairs that led from the basement to the ring and pushed through the door just as Rafferty was about to open it. Delgado knocked him to the ground as he rushed past. In no time, the other dogs were stampeding up behind him.

Chloe was cowering in the corner of the ring as El Diablo crept toward her. Saliva dripped from El Diablo's tongue. "Don't hide over here, *chica*," he jeered. "Let the people see your pretty sweater." He lifted her up by her pink cashmere. It stretched so far that Chloe fell right out of it. Now she was wearing nothing but her diamond-studded collar, which sparkled under the bright lights.

With no other options left, Chloe tried to squeeze through the ring's gate. The crowd howled with laughter when she couldn't fit. El Diablo spit out the sweater, and came back at her, his eyes gleaming with menace.

Chloe whimpered, closed her eyes, and shrank back as far as she could against the gate. She was sure there was no hope for her. But as she leaned against the exit, she felt it shift. Suddenly, the gate lifted and Chloe tumbled out!

She was on the floor outside the ring and Delgado was looking down at her. "Move it!" he hissed. *"Corre!"*

She jumped to her feet just in time to see El Diablo leaping straight at her. But in an instant, Delgado closed the gate on him, leaving him howling in pain and fury. El Diablo was now alone in the ring.

The audience roared for more, thinking it

was part of the show. But all bets were off for the night, because Delgado was leading all the dogs that had followed him from the basement out through a back door.

Chloe couldn't make sense of it all. She just followed Delgado and the others into the streets of Mexico City. It seemed that this was her only hope. With a quick glance backward, she saw that Vasquez and Rafferty were coming after them.

The dogs raced past a busy street market, toppling fruit and startling vendors as they went. Chloe lost a bootie in one of the many mud puddles they ran through, but Delgado wouldn't let her go back for it. Instead, he scooped her up by the collar and sailed with her over a six-foot-high chain-link fence. It was only when they'd landed that Chloe saw that he'd saved her yet again. Vasquez and Rafferty, plus a bunch of other thugs, were glowering at them from the other side of the fence, unable to make their way over it.

Delgado, Chloe, and the rest of the dogs were safe—for now.

Chloe had a hard time keeping up with Delgado as he led the way through the night. Her fur was dirty, and her feet were tired— she had to take four steps for each one of the German shepherd's. To make matters worse, she was sure she was starting to see things! Up ahead, it looked as if human skeletons were playing drums and blocking their path.

"Watch what you're doing," Delgado said as a skeleton almost stepped on Chloe. That's when Chloe realized the skeletons weren't a figment of her imagination. There was a line of them stretching as far as she could see, holding lanterns high as they marched in some kind of parade.

"What is all this?" asked Chloe, not sure if she really wanted to know.

Delgado's voice was hushed. "It's what the humans here do to honor their ancestors," he said. "It keeps them alive in their hearts. Helps them remember who they are, where they came from . . ." Delgado was describing the Mexican feast, *El Dia de los Muertos*, the Day of the Dead. Chloe had never heard of the holiday. She didn't get it, really, but it seemed to mean something to Delgado.

As the parade passed by, the street opened up again, and the dogs began to take off in different directions, saying *"Hasta la vista, chica,"* and, *"Gracias,* Delgado.*"*

Finally, Delgado said to Chloe, "I'll see ya. *Buena suerte."* He was halfway down a dark street before Chloe stopped him.

"'See ya'? That's it?" she demanded. She tried not to show how scared she was.

"Number one rule of the streets, *Princesa*: every dog for himself. Now get lost," he said as he continued down the road.

Tears clouded Chloe's eyes as she tried to catch up with him. "My name's not *Princesa*. It's Chloe and . . . I am lost. I want to be found." Chloe hated it, but she knew she was about to cry.

"Look, kid, I've got my own problems," Delgado replied wearily. "I can't go back to the fights. I gotta get outta town."

Chloe raced under his legs to get in front of him again. "How does Beverly Hills sound?" she suggested boldly.

"Too far," said Delgado.

"Come on," Chloe begged. "If you could figure out a way back, you could live with us on our estate."

Delgado couldn't help smiling. "In case you haven't noticed, I'm a little large for a lapdog."

"But you're the perfect size for a guard dog," Chloe pointed out. "And our old one ran off with a shih tzu."

Finally, Delgado was listening. Guard dog was a job he could handle. He considered the idea for a moment. "What hotel were you staying at?" he asked her.

Chloe jumped for joy. "You'll do it?" she yipped.

"Just answer the question before I change my mind."

"I don't know the name," Chloe admitted. "But believe me, it was no Four Seasons."

Delgado was thinking fast now. "Four Seasons? There's one here. Would they know you?"

"They should," said Chloe proudly. "We're preferred guests. We have a Gold Card."

It wasn't much of a plan, but it was all they had for now. Delgado led the way as Chloe limped behind him. She was ready for a long nap and a massage, but it didn't look like that would happen anytime soon.

CHAPTER FOUR

Back at the warehouse, Vasquez glared at Rafferty and his other thugs. "Tonight was an embarrassment," he said angrily.

"I'm sorry, Senor Vasquez," Rafferty replied. "I was sure I locked those cages."

Vasquez tossed Chloe's torn pink sweater to his accomplice. "Look at that label," he demanded. "I want that Chihuahua."

"Pucci's of Beverly Hills," read Rafferty. He had no clue what it meant.

"She's worth something," Vasquez explained impatiently. "And judging by the bling around her neck, it's a lot."

Rafferty took El Diablo out of his corral and secured a GPS collar to his neck. Then he handed Chloe's pink sweater to the dog. They would watch El Diablo on a GPS monitor as he searched the city for Chloe's scent.

"El Diablo," ordered Vasquez, "bring me the Chihuahua." The Doberman took a deep whiff of the sweater and then tore it to shreds. He let out a primal howl and took off downtown.

Many blocks away, Delgado's ears pricked up. He had heard El Diablo's howl, and he knew what it meant.

With no warning, he pushed Chloe into a filthy puddle almost as deep as she was tall. "Ugh!" sputtered Chloe. "What did you do that for?" She had never been so dirty in her life.

43

"El Diablo's got your scent," Delgado said.

"Well, of course he does," said Chloe pertly. "It's Chanel No. 5. Or it *was*. Now I stink."

"Smell fine to me," Delgado muttered.

"Then you need to get your nose checked," Chloe shot back.

They kept on walking in silence. Chloe hoped they'd reach safety soon.

In the meantime, Rachel had sent her friends home and made her way to Mexico City. She sat in a police station that was full of tourists, scared crime victims, handcuffed criminals, and exhausted cops. A detective named Ramirez managed to pay attention to her in spite of it all.

"What she really is, is selfish," Rachel ranted. "She doesn't care about anybody else's feelings. Really, it's unbelievable."

Finally, the detective stopped her. "Look, *Senorita* Ashe, I'm sorry. We're already trying to stop the fights. And we don't have time to look for every lost dog in Mexico."

Rachel couldn't help rolling her eyes. This was the whole problem, right here. "She's not just any dog," she emphasized. "She's my *aunt's* dog. Her whole life. Chloe means everything to her."

She had worn him down, she could tell. "I'll tell you what," said Detective Ramirez. "Go back to your hotel, download that photo you were telling me about, and I'll see what I can do in the morning."

For a second, Rachel was happy. And then her phone rang. She looked at the number and panicked. "Oh, no!" she cried. "Okay. *Gracias*," she said to the detective before sprinting out the door. She had to be alone to take this call.

Rachel took a deep breath and answered the phone. "Hi, Aunt Viv!' she said with as much enthusiasm as she could muster.

"Darling, where are you?" Viv asked. Rachel knew her aunt was in Rome now, but she sounded much closer, and she sounded worried. "I've been trying the house. . . ."

Rachel did her best to soothe her aunt's concerns. "I, uh . . . Chloe wanted to go out to dinner so we're having . . . Mexican."

The Four Seasons was a cool oasis in the middle of the city's dark and dirty sprawl. Light from its windows bathed the street in a welcoming glow. Chloe had a new burst of energy when she rounded a corner and saw the place. This was almost as good as arriving home.

"Thanks, Delgado," she said. "It won't be long now." She was ready to run inside—until she took a good look at her companion. He was huge and kind of smelly . . . "But maybe you should wait outside," she added. "I don't mean it like it sounds. They can be a little particular about the dogs they let in here."

She nodded at the ornate entrance to the hotel and its uniformed doorman, and Delgado understood what she was saying. He plunked down on the ground to wait for her to return.

Gulping in the cool, clean air, Chloe pranced up to the door and trotted inside as the doorman held it open for an extravagantly dressed couple. She strode across the marble floor to the desk clerk and gave him one of her patented cute looks, her head tilted to one side and eyes big. "If you could be so kind as to look at my collar," she yipped, "you'll find my owner's name and number on the tag."

A Maltese that was passing by at that moment didn't notice Chloe and bumped into her by accident. "Eeeew! It touched me!" he shrieked, edging away. Chloe looked around for a minute before she realized he was talking about her!

"Ugh, how horrible," said the dog's owner, looking Chloe up and down with disgust. "Get this mutt out of here!"

"Mutt!" cried Chloe. "I have been a preferred customer of this hotel for years!"

The desk clerk came around and bent to pick up Chloe. "Don't you dare! You, sir, are making a terrible mistake!" she cried. But the clerk wasn't interested. He didn't know or care what she was saying. Gently, he carried her to a service door and scooted her out into the back alley.

Delgado was tired of waiting. For a while, he had watched people go in and out of the hotel. Then he decided to take a peek inside. He pressed his nose against the window and spotted a Chihuahua sitting alone at a table and being doted on by a waiter.

"Figures," he said to himself, thinking the dog was Chloe. "What did I expect from a *chica* like her?" He was out of there in a heartbeat.

Chloe managed to choke back her tears until she caught a glimpse of herself in the hotel's stainless-steel door. Now that she saw the state she was in it was no wonder the Maltese thought she was a stray. "Oh, no," she whispered to herself, "I'm hideous!"

Heaving great sobs that wracked her tiny body, Chloe made her way back to the front door. But Delgado wasn't there. She was disappointed but not entirely surprised. Nothing else was going her way, so it made sense that Delgado wouldn't bother to stick around.

Now, for the first time in her entire life, Chloe Winthrop Ashe was truly alone. With a sad glance back at the Four Seasons—the last vestige of her old world—she wandered off into the night.

CHAPTER SIX

Early the next morning, Rachel marched back to the police station. This time she was armed with renewed determination. "I need to see the detective," she told the desk sergeant when she arrived.

"Detective Ramirez is already with some-one, *senorita*," the sergeant said politely, before turning to the next person in line.

But today Rachel wasn't taking no for an answer. As soon as the sergeant was distracted, Rachel slipped quietly through the door behind him.

She couldn't believe her eyes. Detective Ramirez wasn't even there. But Aunt Viv's gardener *was*. With his dog, no less!

The last time Rachel had seen this guy, he was digging a koi pond and she was in her pajamas, complaining about the noise. Rachel was totally confused. "You?" she stammered. "What are you doing here? I mean . . . *Que* . . . are you doing here?"

Sam replied in perfect English. "Isn't it obvious?" he said. "I'm here to find Chloe. Your friend Angela told me everything."

Now Rachel was turning red—and not because Angela had spilled the beans when she got back home. She'd always assumed the landscaper didn't speak English—but he obviously did. She started to apologize for trying to speak to him in her terrible Spanish, but Sam interrupted her.

"I'm not here for you, I'm here for Vivian.

Do you have any idea how devastated she'll be?" Sam said.

Detective Ramirez returned at that moment, speaking to Sam. "I e-mailed a description of the dog's collar to all our precincts. They'll get it out to pawnshops in their areas."

"Chloe's collar. It's worth a fortune," Rachel thought aloud. She had to hand it to Sam—that was a good idea.

"You're welcome," Sam said smugly.

Rachel continued. "Well, then perhaps a picture of the collar might be even more helpful." She handed the detective one of her flyers.

"Yeah, a lot," he said.

"Great," Rachel replied crisply. "So what else can we do?"

"We?" the detective asked. "Nothing. I'll e-mail this to all our stations. You go back to your hotel and wait."

When the policeman left the room, Sam

turned to Rachel. "He's right," he said, his tone gentler now. "Come on."

But Rachel wouldn't give up. "He only cares about the collar," she told him. "I need the dog." She stood up and opened the door, leaving Sam at the desk. Then Sam's dog, Papi, leaped up, barking.

"I'm with her, amigo. My Chloe is in trouble," said Papi. Sam was outnumbered. He had no choice but to follow.

It had been the hardest night of Chloe's life. When she finally came across a large park, she decided to find a place to rest. The park was full of shadows and noises that Chloe couldn't identify. It was the kind of place she'd only seen in nightmares, but she lacked the energy to go even one step farther. She limped to a park bench, planning to lay out there in the open, regardless of the danger. But something better was underneath the bench—a cardboard box! Chloe didn't think she'd ever been so happy. She tossed and turned and eventually fell into a deep and dreamless sleep.

In the morning, Chloe woke to the sound of a family walking by. A kid threw a half-eaten churro at a trash can next to Chloe's bench, but it missed and fell into the dirt next to Chloe.

Chloe's mouth began to water. She couldn't remember the last time she'd eaten. It almost didn't matter that the churro was someone else's trash, laden with someone else's germs and lying on the ground. She closed her eyes and opened her mouth to take a bite.

"That's our churro," snarled a dog. Chloe looked up. Suddenly she was surrounded by a gang of stray dogs. She bristled. These dogs were scary, but her growling stomach was scarier. "Excuse me, but I saw it first!" she informed them.

The gang leader took a good look at Chloe, who wasn't exactly at her best. "Ooh, better back off, *muchachos*," he mocked. "Looks like we found one of those Chihuahua warriors."

The other dogs cracked up laughing. One called out, "Please, Senorita Warrior, don't unleash that famous Chihuahua bark on us."

They closed in on Chloe, but she didn't even care. They were *not* going to get away with this—not after what she'd been through.

"Hey, look," she told the closest dog, all business. "I've been dognapped, lost my favorite cashmere sweater, and slept in a box. Plus, I'm starting another in a series of bad hair days. So *don't . . . push me!*" She leaped onto a bench to look him in the eye, and it seemed to do the trick. The dogs took a step back, and Chloe added a growl for good measure.

At that, the dogs fled. Chloe smiled to herself. "That's what I thought." She felt pretty good—and she was ready to dig into that tasty churro.

Chloe hopped off the bench and picked up

her prize. But as she turned to find a quiet place to eat, she saw what the other dogs had *really* been running from. El Diablo stood there, huge and sinister, and his eyes were locked on Chloe from across the path.

"*Que te pasa, chiquita?*" El Diablo asked her in a low growl as he edged toward her. This time Chloe's defenses failed her and she stood paralyzed as the Doberman closed in.

Just then, Chloe saw a blur in the corner of her eye. It shot toward her, grabbed her by the collar, and ran off in the other direction. It was Delgado!

They tore across the park and away from El Diablo. But she heard him calling to Delgado as they ran. "Still trying to be the hero, aren't you?" But Delgado seemed not to hear and just kept running.

The German shepherd raced through traffic and crowded sidewalks. When he reached the center of the city, he crossed the green expanse of Chapultepec Park and headed straight toward Chapultepec Castle. As they barreled through the gates, Chloe heard a man speaking to a group of tourists. "The Aztec Empire spread all over Mexico, but its heart was right here in Mexico City. You are in Chapultepec Park, once used by Mexican kings as a royal retreat. . . ." Chloe loved castles. But this castle was a museum, and she wasn't likely to get pampered here.

Still carrying Chloe, Delgado burst into the opulent Aztec History Hall and slid on his toenails across the polished floor. He flew through a tour group and past a model of the Aztec Empire, sliding at last into a large stone block from an Aztec pyramid. At the moment they finally stopped moving, Chloe could see that the stone was carved with hieroglyphs—one of which featured a king and his Chihuahua! How appropriate, she thought, preening for a second.

But before she knew it, El Diablo skidded into the hall, too. He gave an earsplitting howl, and the tourists scattered. Delgado made a run for it, heading up a staircase. A security guard chased them, but he was no match for a German shepherd at top speed.

On tiptoe, Delgado led Chloe into an upstairs exhibit. A diorama showed Cortés, his soldiers, and their Spanish dogs meeting the Aztecs and their Chihuahuas for the first time. Delgado froze beside the Spanish troops, trying to fit in, while Chloe faced him, utterly still beside a model of an Aztec warrior.

"Why did you abandon me?" Chloe asked Delgado in a whisper. "I've already been abandoned once!"

"*You* left *me*," accused Delgado. "I saw you in there getting pampered."

Chloe had no idea what he was talking about. "The closest thing I got to food was a used churro . . ." She broke off as the guard made his way down the hall and into the room with the diorama. Chloe held her breath as he looked at the display suspiciously. But he finally moved away, scratching his head.

Suddenly, the guard blew his whistle and took off after something down the hall. From the sound of the footsteps, Chloe could tell it was El Diablo—and she was pretty sure *he* wouldn't miss them in the diorama! Delgado leaped out of the exhibit, motioning for her to follow, and they flew toward the stairs at the other end of the hall. Delgado stood on his hind legs and pressed the bar of the door to the stairs with his paws. They took the stairs three at a time, all the way down. Behind them, El Diablo had been caught and was being restrained by the guards.

"Where are we going now?" Chloe asked wearily.

"I'm taking you to Puerto Vallarta," Delgado announced. "There's someone there who can help us."

CHAPTER SEVEN

Chloe and Delgado made their way back through the city. They knew they were safe from El Diablo, but they couldn't resist the urge to constantly look behind them. Eventually, Delgado led the way as they jumped into the back of a flatbed truck. The two dogs hunkered down between some crates as the truck shuddered to life and hit the road.

Chloe decided to try and clear some things up. "Why is El Diablo after me?" she asked. Last she heard, dogfights stopped in the ring.

"Vasquez must have sent him," Delgado guessed.

"Who's Vasquez?"

"He runs the dogfights and anything else he can make a buck at. The police have been after him for years, but he's too slippery," Delgado explained.

"How do you know all that?" Chloe demanded, suddenly curious. "Were you a criminal or something?" Delgado had been good to her, it was true. But she really didn't know a thing about him.

Delgado said, "Or something," and left it at that.

There was one more thing Chloe wanted to know. "What did El Diablo mean by 'Still trying to be the hero'?"

Delgado yawned and turned away to go to sleep without answering.

Rachel, Sam, and Papi combed the streets for any evidence that Chloe had been there.

Their first big break came at the street market. Papi dug furiously at something in the gutter, then danced in front of Sam with it in his teeth.

"Chloe's bootie!" Rachel cried.

"She is near. I can feel it!" Papi rejoiced. He was clearly more in love than ever.

Sam had even more good news. "This vendor says a Chihuahua was in a pack of dogs that escaped the fights two days ago," he told Rachel. "She was being carried by a German shepherd. He helped her get away."

A Chihuahua being carried sounded just like Chloe. It had to be her!

Unfortunately, Rachel and Sam weren't the only people searching for Chloe.

Rafferty found one of Rachel's flyers and brought it to Vasquez. A little Internet search of the information on the flyer revealed all he needed to know: Chloe belonged to one very rich woman! "There's a lot of money riding on

It's just another day in the fabulous life of Vivian Ashe—and her Chihuahua, Chloe!

Chloe meets Vivian's niece Rachel for lunch.

After a tough day of shopping, Chloe unwinds by the pool
with her friends.

Papi thinks Chloe is the dog of his dreams—she's
not so sure.

Rachel is thrilled to be in Mexico with her friends. There's
no *way* she's going to let Chloe cramp her style.

When Chloe sneaks out of the hotel room, she ends up lost.

Chloe finds herself facing something even scarier than being lost—the dogfighter El Diablo.

Chloe has escaped the dogfights, but now she has to spend the night alone in a park.

Papi and his owner, Vivian's landscaper Sam, come to Mexico to help Rachel find Chloe.

Chloe and Delgado find themselves at a Chihuahua temple.

Margarita tells Chloe about her ancestry and about
Chihuahuas' role in history.

Sam, Papi, and Rachel finally find Chloe. But did
they find her in time?

Now that Chloe has found her bark, she's ready to take
on anything with her new friends!

her," Vasquez declared. "They can't find the dog before we do!"

At dawn, the truck carrying Chloe and Delgado arrived in the elegant port town of Puerto Vallarta. When the flatbed truck stopped for a light, the dogs hopped out. Chloe followed Delgado to a fountain in the town's central square.

"Plant your paws here, keep your muzzle shut, and wait for me to come back," Delgado told Chloe firmly.

She didn't argue, but she wouldn't have minded knowing where he was going—or when he was coming back. But for a dog who was desperately in need of a bath, a fountain was a good place to wait. Chloe sighed with relief and submerged herself in the water, gazing at the brilliant blue sky and dreaming of the pool back home. When the grime and muck had washed away, she stepped delicately out of the fountain and shook herself off, her diamond collar glinting in the sun. Chloe had just curled up to take a nap when she heard a voice in distress nearby.

"Help! Please, help me! Somebody!" It was a pack rat, struggling to free himself from an iguana's mouth.

"Who? Me? What do I do?" Chloe wanted to help, but how? The iguana looked dangerous.

The rat was now halfway down the iguana's throat. "Something! Anything!" he screamed.

Tentatively, Chloe shouted "Uh, shoo, lizard, shoo—" To her surprise, the iguana spit out the rat with a look of fright and ran away into the crowd!

The rat lay next to the fountain with his eyes closed, motionless. Chloe poked him with her paw. "Oh, my gosh," she said. "Are you all right? Hello? *Hola*?"

Coughing so hard his eyes bulged out, the rat woke up. When he saw Chloe, he froze. "Are you an angel?" he asked suspiciously. "Am I dead?"

Chloe smiled. "No. And I'm not an angel."

The rat was mesmerized by her collar. "And yet you are wearing a halo."

It had been a long time since anyone had paid Chloe a compliment. "This?" she said, craning her neck so he could see it better. "It's my collar from Van Cleef & Arpels."

"Is that in heaven?" the rat asked.

"Well, sort of." Chloe sighed. "Beverly Hills."

Suddenly the rat looked concerned. "You're a long way from home," he said gently. "Perhaps I can be of assistance." He bowed with a flourish and boasted, "I am Manuel. I work on a luxury cruise ship as a porter, tending to the discriminating needs of refined, upscale dogs like yourself."

"Really?" Chloe gasped. "Do you think you could help me get home?"

"You saved my life," said Manuel. "It's the very least I can do."

CHAPTER EIGHT

Delgado was standing outside a police-dog training school, looking longingly through the fence. He remembered how it felt to fly through the obstacle course, scrambling over the wall and weaving skillfully through the cones.

Just as he was about to walk away, too proud to return, he was spotted by an old friend. "Delgado?" said another German shepherd from the other side of the fence. This one was wearing an officer's badge. "It's really you, cuz? What happened? Where have you been? Nobody's seen you since . . . you know, a while."

"I see you made sergeant, Tomas," Delgado said, nodding at the badge his cousin wore.

"Yeah," Tomas said. "I was gettin' a little tired of the field."

Delgado stared at the ground. "I know what you mean." He paused for a moment, then dropped all pretenses. "Look . . . I'm doing a little security gig, taking a rich Chihuahua back to Beverly Hills. She's got a tag on her collar."

"So take her to a rescue shelter," Tomas barked, a bit impatiently. "They can read it and call the owner."

"It's not that simple," Delgado explained. "Vasquez is looking for her, and he's got informants everywhere. He's even got El Diablo out after her."

Tomas grinned knowingly. "El Diablo?" he asked. "That's why you're doing it?"

"That *malhechor*'s behind me," Delgado

promised him. "It's just a job. Can you get Officer Menendez to call her tag?"

After a moment, Tomas nodded. "Bring it to me and I'll see what I can do."

Delgado bounded across the square and stopped at the fountain next to Chloe. "Come on," he said, poking her with his muzzle. "I found someone to read your tag."

"Really?" Chloe said, cocking her head. "Well, so did I."

Delgado stared at the spot on her neck where her collar used to be. "Where's your collar?" he growled.

"You're not the only one who can get things done, you know."

"Gringa loca!" Delgado exclaimed, rolling his eyes. "What did you do?"

Chloe tried to tell Delgado about how she'd saved Manuel from the iguana, but Delgado interrupted before she could finish. "An iguana?" he repeated in disbelief. *"De donde eres!* That's the oldest con in the book! Iguanas are vegetarians!"

Chloe was confused. "I'm sorry, okay?" she retorted. "You don't meet many iguanas on Rodeo Drive." She didn't see why Delgado was so upset. Viv would get her another collar.

"Do you know what you've done?" he snapped. "Without your ID tag, there's nothing to separate you from any collarless stray on the street!"

Chloe slumped against the fountain as she realized what giving up her collar meant. The dogs stood there in silence until Delgado walked away, shaking his head. "This only leaves us one option," he said. After her big mistake, though, Chloe would take whatever she could get. And she knew that if anyone could get her out of this mess, it was Delgado.

In a back alley not far away, Manuel and his accomplice, Chico, were gloating over their latest escapade. Manuel, wearing Chloe's collar as a belt, showed it to Chico behind a grocery store. "You're wearing a halo. That's funny, man," the iguana chortled, remembering what Manuel had said to Chloe at the fountain.

"No, Chico, that's irony . . ." Manuel said to him with a laugh. But he broke off when he caught sight of something terrifying in the corner of his eye.

El Diablo loomed over them—Vasquez must have released him once more. He began snarling, and Chico screamed. The iguana darted behind some trash for cover while El Diablo backed Manuel up against the wall. "Where is the Chihuahua?" the Doberman demanded.

Trying to hide the diamond collar behind him, Manuel stammered, "Chihuahua? I don't know any Chihuahua. I'm from the Yucatán. Of course, if you'd like to meet one, I could arrange it. . . ."

El Diablo leaned in, his bad breath ruffling Manuel's fur. "You're trying my patience, *chaparrito*," he whispered ominously. "Where is she?"

The rat didn't stand a chance against this beast, and he knew it. "By the fountain near the docks," he said, giving in. "I didn't know she was, like, a friend of yours, man. I was . . . just borrowing it." He took the collar from behind his back in a gesture of peace, but El Diablo was already racing away.

He wasn't after the diamonds, Manuel realized. He was after the dog. And heaven help her, wherever she was.

Chloe was picking her way through a rail yard, heading for the freight end of a stopped train. "A coyote?" she asked Delgado. She still wasn't sure she got it.

"A smuggler," he repeated. "They sneak collarless dogs across the border. Follow me." He led the way across a crisscrossing maze of tracks, making sure they steered clear of the trains lumbering heavily into the station.

As she trudged along, Chloe began to put two and two together. "You used to be a police dog, didn't you?" she asked Delgado. "That's how you know that Sergeant Tomas. That's why you can do all those things."

"I don't want to talk about it," Delgado snapped.

But Chloe wasn't letting him off the hook. "Did you quit?"

"What part of 'I don't want to talk about it' did you not understand?"

"If you didn't quit, did you get fired? Did you do something wrong?"

"Yes, I did something wrong," Delgado barked. "Okay? Satisfied? Now let's just drop it!" A train whistle echoed in the silence that followed.

"Okay," said Chloe. For a moment, she was silent, too. But she couldn't help herself. She had to know! "What was it? Was someone hurt?"

Reaching a boxcar at the end of the train,

Delgado stopped suddenly. "*Suficiente!*" he exploded. "You're driving me *loco!*"

"Well, you're not exactly the most charming travel companion, either," retorted Chloe. It wasn't her fault he couldn't open up.

"Then it's good we're parting ways," replied Delgado firmly. Before Chloe could reply, he hopped into the open boxcar and lifted her in after him. "This train'll take you to Tijuana, then you can get over the border from there." With that, Delgado hopped back onto the tracks—and just in time, because the train was beginning to move.

Her heart in her throat, Chloe watched Delgado getting smaller and smaller as the train crawled out of the yard. She was too stunned even to wave good-bye. The coyote was in the shadows behind her, looking ragged and hungry, and the one dog who'd been kind to her since she'd left home was about to drop out of her life for good. *I didn't mean to be rude,* Chloe thought bitterly. *I just wanted to know what was up with him. Was that so wrong?*

But just as the train began to pick up speed, something amazing happened. With no warning at all, Delgado bounded after it! It took everything he had to catch the train and pull himself into the car with Chloe, but he acted like it was no big deal. "I promised I'd get you to Beverly Hills," he panted, as if he'd sworn his life on it.

"Sure thing, Delgado," Chloe chirped. She'd annoyed him, she knew, and she'd made a big mistake by handing her collar off to some stranger. But Delgado was going to stick by her, anyway, it seemed. And maybe— just maybe—he would finally get her home to Viv.

CHAPTER NINE

In Chapultepec Park, Rachel and Sam followed Papi as he zigzagged all over the place, following Chloe's scent. It was here . . . and there . . . as well as all over two mangy dogs. Leaving Rachel and Sam behind, Papi went to investigate.

"You. That scent," Papi said, walking right up to them and sniffing. "Where did you get that scent?"

The dogs were Milagros and Rafa, the pit

bull and the terrier who'd escaped the fights with Delgado and Chloe.

Milagros was confused. "You mean the moldy taco?" he asked.

"No," said Papi impatiently. "The perfume. It's Chloe's. She's an American Chihuahua." How could he describe her? "Her ears are as pink as seashells," he added dreamily. "And her nose is like a raspberry?"

Milagros nodded. "*Espera*," he said. "Is she kind of uppity, wears matching clothes?"

Papi perked up. "You know her! Where is she?"

"Last we saw her, she was with Delgado on the run," Milagros said.

"Delgado? Who is this Delgado?" Papi asked jealously. "I want to hear more. Come with me."

Sam and Rachel were sitting on a bench, exhausted, when Papi appeared with the two dogs. "Looks like we've picked up a couple of friends," Sam commented.

Rachel rolled her eyes. "Great. That's all I need. More strays."

"Hey," said Sam. "Papi was a stray. I saved him from the pound." And even Rachel had to admit that Papi was a special dog—loyal, brave, and friendly.

Just then, Milagros sidled up to Rachel and put his blocky head on her knee, gazing at her with soft, trusting eyes. "Well, he is cute," she said, shaking her head. A friend of Papi's was a friend of hers. And Aunt Viv would have helped the stray dogs without a second thought. "But you have to give them a bath. They stink!"

Back at the hotel, Sam and Rachel got the dogs into the tub, laughing as they dodged wagging tails and flying suds. They'd never paid much attention to each other at Viv's place, but now they were really getting along.

When the baths were done, the two of them got cleaned up and returned to find the three dogs sitting together in the hotel room, gazing out the window. "It's a nice thing you did for them," said Sam, looking over at Rafa and Milagros, who were cleaner than they'd ever been.

Rachel sighed. "I just hope somebody's out there doing the same thing for Chloe."

The train rumbled up the Mexican coastline. Along the way, it had stopped to pick up passengers, and now Chloe and Delgado were traveling with a crowd of Mexican dogs. Delgado was snoring in a corner while Chloe fielded questions from a curious puppy who had joined them.

"What's America like?" he asked her, eyes wide.

"Well, I've been all over," Chloe began, ready to tell the puppy about all the wonders of her life back home. But before she could begin, she was distracted by the moonlight shining on the Mexican landscape. It looked beautiful and strange. "But . . ." she continued, thinking of the way she used to view the world, "I don't think I've ever really seen it." As soon as she said it, she knew it was true.

The puppy didn't get it, but he had other things on his mind—he was staring at her bootie. "What is that?"

"It's a bootie," Chloe explained. "I lost the others. All the dogs in Beverly Hills wear them to protect their feet."

"It must be very dirty there," the puppy said, sounding sorry for the dogs in Beverly Hills.

Chloe laughed. "No, actually, it's probably the cleanest place I know."

The puppy started laughing, too. "Then it's pretty silly to wear booties."

Chloe had never really thought of it that way. "You know something?" she said. "You're right!" She bent over, took the last bootie in her mouth, and hurled it out of the train and into the darkness. For a moment it floated in the air, and then it was whisked away by the wind.

Back in Puerto Vallarta, Manuel and Chico were in a grocery store finishing up a feast. They'd found a piñata full of candy and were enjoying its sugary treats. Surrounded by torn candy wrappers, Manuel loosened the diamond collar around his middle to make himself more comfortable and burped. "Man, that's better," he said. "But maybe we shoulda hit the salad bar."

Suddenly, the floor beneath them seemed to move. Then it came apart completely, and they fell into blinding light! They dropped a long way, finally crashing onto another floor! The tattered remains of the donkey piñata that had housed them only seconds before clattered down around them with a hollow sound.

"Ahhhhh!" screamed a lady staring down

at them. *"Una rata!"* Manuel and Chico made a run for it.

First, a little boy chased them. And then the store owner came after them with a broom! Fearing for his life, Manuel raced as fast as his legs could carry him—and right out of Chloe's collar!

The store owner picked up the collar in amazement. As he stared, mesmerized by the diamonds, Manuel and Chico disappeared.

No matter how hard she tried, Chloe could not get warm in the train. Her teeth were chattering so loudly that she was afraid of waking someone up. As she tried to find a comfortable spot, she felt a tail wrap around her and draw her close. It was Delgado. His tail was warm and soft, and she finally felt comfortable. It seemed like he always knew just what she needed.

As she began to drift off to sleep, the quiet of the nighttime train was shattered by a fearful cry. "The conductor's coming!" a dog hissed. All the dogs in the car rushed for cover, hiding behind crates and boxes so they wouldn't be spotted. Chloe cowered in a corner and waited for the worst. Then she realized that Delgado was still out in the open—no hiding place on this train was big enough for a German shepherd. He caught her eye and whispered, "Don't come out, no matter what happens!"

The conductor opened the door. Before he could begin his inspection, Delgado leaped past him and bounded away in the other direction! The conductor whipped around and chased him.

Chloe and the other dogs crept quietly out of their hiding places. The coast was clear, but the price had been high. They could hear passengers shrieking and luggage flying as Delgado moved through the train like a hurricane.

"Your friend was very brave to lead them

away," a mother dog said to Chloe.

An older dog added, "*Si*. He saved all of us."

Chloe bit her tongue to keep from crying. Delgado had saved her so many times. What was going to happen to him? The train squealed to a stop, and Chloe listened to the shouts of the men as they chased her friend. It was only a matter of time now. What would they do with him if they caught him? And what would Chloe do then?

After a while, Chloe stopped hearing the telltale sounds of a dog on the loose, and the train began to pick up speed again. Chloe stared out the window at the countryside with no idea what to do next. The night had seemed beautiful just minutes before, but now it seemed forbidding. There was nothing to see but fields and sky and—and a German shepherd watching the last car shoot by!

Chloe realized that Delgado had made it off the train! And in a split second, she knew what she had to do. Hoping for the best, she closed her eyes and jumped!

She landed with an "Umph," right at Delgado's feet. "Did you see that?" she cried excitedly. "I just jumped off a train! By myself! And it was moving!"

Delgado seemed stunned. "But I told you to stay aboard!"

"I couldn't just leave you here," Chloe said. "We're in this together. I've never had a friend like you."

She could tell that Delgado was touched, but he tried to cover it up with his usual gruff manner. "You shoulda stayed, kid," he said, shaking his head. "Take a look around."

What Chloe hadn't seen from the train window was a canyon yawning ahead of them, with tall mountains looming all around. Alone, she would have found this scene daunting. But not now. With Delgado, she was ready to face whatever the night might bring.

CHAPTER TEN

As the sun rose higher in the sky, Chloe and Delgado trudged up a dusty trail. They rounded a bend and Chloe, frowning, looked at a squat tree. "We've passed that tree before," she said.

"*Te equivocas,*" Delgado replied. "We've been walking for hours."

Chloe walked up to the tree and sniffed. "I tinkled there. Can't you tell?"

Delgado was irritated. "You don't know

what you're talking about. Pick up the pace," he said sharply.

Rachel and Sam were in Puerto Vallarta with Detective Ramirez, talking to the grocery-store owner who had found Chloe's diamond collar. He returned the collar to Rachel and told them all about finding Manuel and Chico hiding in the piñata. "The rat, he's clever," explained the store owner. "I set traps to keep him out, but he always gets in!"

Rachel smiled, patting Milagros's head with one hand as she placed Chloe's collar into her bag with the other. "What you need is a watchdog," she told him.

The store owner looked the pit bull up and down. "He's a stray," he replied uncertainly.

But Rachel stood her ground. "He may be a stray, but he's a good dog," she insisted. Before long, the store owner had slipped a collar around Milagros's neck, and the other dogs were saying good-bye!

Sam and Rachel led Rafa and Papi outside and walked back to the car they'd rented. Opening the door, Sam said to Rachel, "You're a pretty good matchmaker."

"I didn't do anything," said Rachel, blushing. "It just worked out." It was hard to feel good about anything after losing Aunt Viv's dog! Still, she appreciated that Sam was being nice to her. It was hard to believe now that she'd once thought of him as just "the gardener."

Detective Ramirez came out of the store. He'd been taking a call. "That was the Puerto Vallarta police," he said. "There was some dog trouble on a northbound train this morning. A German shepherd jumped off . . ."

Sam and Rachel answered at the same time. "Chloe!"

As they rushed away, two sets of eyes watched from behind a trash can.

The rat, Manuel, muttered, "Man, she's getting away with my collar."

"I think that's, like, karma, man," said

87

Chico. "You steal it, it's stolen from you—"

"—I steal it back," Manuel added.

Chico stared at him in surprise. "How you gonna do that?"

Chloe and Delgado trudged wearily around a bend until Delgado's steps slowed to a dead stop. Chloe looked at him and followed his gaze to that same squat tree with two sets of footprints—his and hers—leading up to it.

"See!" she cried. "I *told* you we'd been here before! Our scent is all over . . ." Then suddenly she realized what had to be wrong. "Oh, my. You can't smell, can you?"

Delgado wouldn't meet her gaze.

"What happened?" Chloe asked in a near whisper. "It's okay. You can tell me."

"I didn't quit the police force," Delgado said flatly. "They let me go because I could no longer follow a scent. And now we're out here walking in circles."

Chloe could tell Delgado felt as if it was all

his fault that they were lost. To make matters worse, she could hear a menacing growl in the distance. "Mountain lions," Delgado announced. "We better get moving."

They headed up the side of a canyon, and Chloe detected movement above them. "Delgado, they're following us," she said nervously.

"I know," he replied. "We've gotta get out of the open."

He led Chloe into the mouth of a cave, just as the sun disappeared behind the mountains. Chloe was scared and a little cold, but for once she wasn't thinking only of herself. She wanted to hear more of Delgado's story. "What happened to you? Why can't you smell anything?" There had to be a reason.

For a moment, she wasn't sure Delgado would answer. Then a faraway look came over his face as he told her about being part of a major bust. He'd led his partner into a dark, abandoned building, when a large shape flew out of the darkness and toppled him over. In a blinding flash of gunfire, Delgado had seen the leering face of the dog who'd knocked him down. It was El Diablo. Delgado got to his feet only to discover that everything had changed.

"While I was lying there, my partner took a bullet and the perps got away. Next day, I woke up, couldn't smell a thing," said Delgado.

"You were hurt?" Chloe asked gently.

Delgado shook his head no. "They say it's all in my head." But obviously he didn't agree.

While Chloe took this in, she could hear growls echoing all around the cave. Delgado stood up purposefully. "They've found us," he said. "I'll hold them off as long as I can while you run."

Chloe wasn't sure what scared her more—being eaten by mountain lions or escaping the mountain lions *without* Delgado.

"They're just cats, you can take 'em," she

chirped, hoping to cheer him up. "I can't make it on my own."

But Delgado was clearly bothered by the memory of the day he lost his sense of smell. "We'd need a miracle," he sighed. Chloe crept to the cave's mouth and dared to glance outside. Just as she'd suspected, the hungry mountain lions were right there, waiting. She felt paralyzed, but Delgado barked fiercely and urged her on. "Now! Run, kid! *Corre!*"

Delgado and Chloe ran for their lives, but the beasts were close behind them. Suddenly, there was a low rumbling in the distance. It grew even louder, and a cloud of dust blew up from every direction. Completely overwhelmed, Delgado, Chloe, and the mountain lions stopped and looked around. When the dust cleared, Chloe spotted the toughest, meanest looking pack of wild Chihuahuas she could imagine.

From the center of the pack, a tiny dog marched up to the mountain lions and grinned. "Say hello to my little friends," he taunted. All at once, the Chihuahuas began to bark. It was hard to believe that such little dogs could produce such a deafening roar, but in no time the noise sent the mountain lions fleeing into the distance.

Once the cats were gone, the warrior Chihuahua turned to Delgado and Chloe, who were standing in silent shock. "I am Montezuma," he proclaimed, "king of the Chihuahuas. Come with us if you want to live."

While Delgado stood there speechless, Chloe murmured, "It's a miracle."

CHAPTER ELEVEN

Chloe and Delgado followed Montezuma and the warriors down a trail. They turned around a bend to see a lush, green valley nestled in a canyon. Rising from a stream were the ruins of an ancient city. This was the home of the warrior Chihuahuas.

Chloe had never seen anything like it. "Where are we?" she asked Montezuma.

"You are in Chihuahua," said the king. "This is Techichi, birthplace of our mighty breed." He sounded surprised that Chloe needed to be told this.

"Uh, I was born in Beverly Hills," Chloe said in explanation. This was a strange land, but as Montezuma and his guests were greeted by dozens of Chihuahuas, Chloe felt oddly at ease. "I feel like I've been here before," she whispered to Delgado.

"You're just dehydrated," he muttered. But she didn't allow his sour comment to diminish her sense of wonder.

"You can rest here before the feast," said Montezuma.

"What feast?" asked Chloe. She was sure she would have remembered if he'd told her about *that* before—she was starving.

The king looked at her quizzically. "In honor of the full moon," he explained. "Like our ancestors before us." When he saw Chloe's blank look, he smiled and added, "I see you have much to learn. And please, call me Monte."

As the dogs waited for the sun to set and the moon to rise, the Chihuahuas did their best to make Chloe and Delgado feel comfortable. One graying, old dog set a bowl in front of Chloe, and she reached her paws out eagerly to eat, stopping short when she realized it was filled with a bunch of grasshoppers!

Chloe cringed, but Delgado was amused. "Eat it," he nudged her, "or you'll offend them." Chloe could see that everyone was watching. They had rescued her, after all— she wanted to be polite. Gingerly, she picked up a grasshopper and took the tiniest bite she could manage, pretending she was back at the Four Seasons.

She chewed and realized that the grasshopper had a satisfying crunch.

In fact, grasshoppers weren't so bad.

"It's tasty!" she exclaimed, suddenly remembering when Papi had given her that grasshopper back at Viv's estate. "I didn't know . . ." she said under her breath. "I . . . never even gave it a chance."

She and Papi were different, but they were both Chihuahuas. Chloe couldn't help but wonder what he would make of this place. Suddenly, she wished she'd been nicer to him—now he probably wouldn't even want to talk to her again. If she ever got home, that was.

Monte noticed her letting out a long breath. "Is something wrong?" he asked with concern.

"No," said Chloe, shaking her head. "I was just thinking of . . . home. Someone from home, really. A Chihuahua who's different from me."

Monte gestured to all the faces around them and explained, "We Chihuahuas come in many shapes and colors. But when you look not with your eyes, but with your soul—there, we're all the same."

Maybe it was true, Chloe thought. It had

never occurred to her that she and Papi had anything in common. What was it that he was always calling her? When she remembered, she asked Monte about it. *"Mi corazon,"* she said. "What does that mean?"

"My heart," said Monte.

Chloe's eyes widened in surprise. Papi had been trying to tell her something, and she'd never even heard him.

Another long day drew to a close, and Sam pulled the rental car into the dusty parking lot of the only inn in a desolate Mexican town.

Staring straight ahead, Rachel asked, "Why are we stopping?"

Sam sighed. "The sun will be down soon, and this is the last town for miles. We can't go all night."

"That's just great," Rachel shot back, starting to lose her cool. "My aunt's due back in two days. I've lost the most precious thing in

97

her life. And now we're stopping in the middle of nowhere."

But Sam was patient. "Rachel," he said, "it's okay. You're doing your best. We're gonna find Chloe."

Rachel took a deep breath and climbed out of the car. It was a lucky thing Sam was there, she thought. She wasn't sure she could do this without him.

As soon as Rachel and Sam were out of sight, the zipper on Rachel's suitcase slid open and Manuel poked out his head!

Manuel eyed Rachel's purse, which was out in the open. "There's the bag that's got my collar!" he crowed. He stepped out of the suitcase and toward the front seat. Chico was right behind him. But just as he prepared to dive into the purse, a dog jumped up from the floor!

"You're the pack rat who stole the collar," Papi snarled, baring his teeth.

"Oh, man, we're busted," Chico commented.

"You've got me mixed up with another rat, man," Manuel told the Chihuahua. "You know, we all look alike."

But Chico couldn't take it. "He's lying!" he shouted. "We did it! We give up!"

"And now the love of my life is out there in trouble," Papi growled.

Manuel rushed to get a few more words in before the dog attacked. "But not because of us," he babbled. "We were just trying to save her from the demon dog who's hunting her."

Narrowing his eyes, Papi said, "Tell me about this demon dog."

CHAPTER TWELVE

The full moon was high in the sky, glowing and brilliant. In the center of Techichi, the Chihuahuas were gathered around a pool that reflected its light and beauty. Chloe sat at the edge of the water, facing Monte, ready to be initiated into an ancient ritual.

"This water comes from a spring hidden deep in Techichi," Monte explained. "Your ancestors drank from it, Chloe of Beverly Hills. Now it is your turn to join with the past."

With all the Chihuahuas watching, Chloe

sipped from the pool. "Now, Chihuahua, learn what you're made of," Monte commanded.

"But I don't understand," Chloe protested. She felt the same as she had before she drank the water. Then, before her eyes, the world morphed into an ancient Aztec battlefield.

"What's happening?" Chloe asked, her voice trembling. "Am I dreaming?" She was on the sidelines of a fierce fight between the Aztecs and their enemies. A large human warrior fell to the ground next to her, almost crushing Chloe.

Before she could even scream, a cream-colored Chihuahua raced to her side. "This is no dream, Chloe!" the Chihuahua shouted. "Follow me!" Chloe stayed close to her as she dodged flying axes and the legs of fighting soldiers in combat above her. Finally, the dog led her to cover behind a rock in the middle of the field.

"Who are you?" Chloe asked, almost afraid to know the answer.

"I am Margarita," the other Chihuahua said. "My bloodline runs in your veins. The blood of warriors. It is your heritage."

Chloe was embarrassed. She knew this couldn't be true. "But I'm just a lapdog," she tried to explain.

"You are much more than that," Margarita said.

Chloe looked around and saw the Aztec king fighting, a proud Chihuahua in warrior headdress at his feet. "Who's that?" she asked a little skeptically. Where she came from, nobody would wear a hat like that.

"The first Chihuahua warrior, Montezuma, like *our* king," Margarita said with pride. "He accompanied the ancient king everywhere, even to the underworld." As Chloe and Margarita looked on, the Chihuahua barked a warning to the king, who deflected the spear of his opponent just in time! The king thanked the Chihuahua and raised his arms in joyful victory.

"Would you like to see more?" Margarita asked. Reading the look on Chloe's face, she whisked her to a maze deep within an Aztec pyramid. "These tunnels were built especially for Chihuahuas," Margarita told Chloe. "Our tiny size can be an advantage."

Next, they visited the royal chamber of the pyramid, where a Chihuahua delivered a secret note from a servant to the princess he loved. "A love none would know about," Margarita said. "Chihuahuas were the only trusted messengers."

"But she's a princess and he's just . . . a servant," Chloe said with wonder.

Margarita gave Chloe a knowing look. "True love sees only what is in the heart," she replied.

"Mi corazon . . ." Chloe said quietly as they left the room.

Leading Chloe through an ordinary Aztec village, Margarita pointed out something else. "We did not have to be royal to be heroes," she said. The two dogs watched a Chihuahua lunge at a snake just as it slithered into the basket of a sleeping baby.

"He saved the child's life!" Chloe marveled.

"Chihuahuas protected all the Aztec people," Margarita said. "Though our bodies appear small, on the inside we are mighty."

Chloe paused thoughtfully. "I never knew we could do all those things," she said. Margarita's face grew dark, her voice intense. "You were guided to Techichi for that reason," she said. "You are nearing the end of your journey, but there is still great danger ahead. It is you, and only you, Chloe, who can save yourself and others."

"How?" asked Chloe, overwhelmed.

Margarita put her paw on Chloe's. "You must find your bark and unleash the Chihuahua within. Only then will you see that your true size is as big as your spirit."

"But what does that mean?" Chloe cried,

almost desperately. What was Margarita talking about?

But her guide had begun to fade into thin air, like a ghost. "Come back, Margarita! Come back!" Chloe cried.

All she heard in return was a thin echo: "I am always with you, *Adelita*. . . ."

CHAPTER THIRTEEN

Delgado watched intently as Chloe sat in a trance before the pool of water. He waved a paw in front of her face, but she didn't even blink. He was getting worried that she might not wake up at all when her limbs began to stir. Delgado wasn't sure what to make of it, but Monte acted like he'd seen this kind of thing before.

"The first time is something, *verdad*? Who came to you?" Monte asked as Chloe's eyes fluttered open.

"Margarita," Chloe said, a glazed look on her face.

"Ah," breathed Monte. "You have been honored. She was a great warrior princess." He stopped and thought for a second. "From now on, you shall bear the ancient Chihuahua name—"

Chloe interrupted. *"Adelita."* Suddenly she understood Margarita's parting words as well as she understood the routines of a day spa. They were an indelible part of her now. "What does it mean, though?" she asked Monte.

"Female warrior," he told her.

"But what will I fight?"

A smile broke over Monte's face. "You will know when the time comes."

Just then, a grizzled, old Chihuahua looked up at the glowing moon and said, "We're ready, King Monte."

Monte looked to the heavens. "We are Chihuahuas! Hear us roar!" he proclaimed.

All the dogs gathered, threw their heads back, and together let loose a mighty bark. It was just like the bark that saved Chloe and Delgado from the mountain lions, only louder. And the sound was full of heart and soul.

Swept away by the sound and the energy in the air, Chloe tried to join the barking. At first she managed only her usual yip and, glancing around, she hoped that nobody had heard her meager voice. After that, taking a deep breath, she let loose her first real bark! It blended in with the other dogs' strong voices, and, for just a moment, Chloe could have sworn her voice made the moon shine brighter.

The next morning, the sky filled with rosy light as the Chihuahuas gathered to wish Chloe and Delgado farewell. Before they left, Monte took Chloe aside. "You can always stay here with us," he said.

Looking out over the ancient city, Chloe sighed. "This place is amazing, Monte," she said slowly. "But there are people and friends back home who'd miss me. And I'd miss them, too."

Monte nodded in understanding. He gave Delgado directions—they were to follow the canyon north to a river. The river would lead them to the ocean. They would know where to go from there. Monte turned to Chloe as she and Delgado began to take their leave. "Wherever you go, always remember where you came from and who you are."

Chloe thought about that as she walked. She was a mighty Chihuahua, not just a lapdog far from home.

Chloe and Delgado made their way through the blazing desert, and Chloe didn't utter a single complaint. But when the path beside the river was blocked by a sheer cliff wall she felt her strength of spirit waver.

"Now, how do we follow the river?" Chloe wanted to know.

Delgado looked at the water and then back at Chloe. "Well, do you swim?" he asked.

For a moment, Chloe could picture the cool water in Viv's pool. "Yes," she said wistfully, "but only with my water *wiiiings!*" Before she knew what had happened, Chloe was flying through the air and into the river. Delgado had shoved her off the riverbank and jumped in after her!

The two dogs floated quickly downstream. Soon the desert landscape turned to dense jungle. And when they rounded a bend, a sign indicated that they'd made it into Basaseachi National Park. Chloe was relieved to see obvious signs of civilization, but a moment later she saw that they were about to fly over a waterfall!

Chloe climbed onto Delgado's back and held on for dear life. "Okay, you can take it from here," she told her friend.

Bravely, Delgado paddled through the surging current and climbed onto the riverbank. The two soaked dogs shook themselves dry and headed straight for the ranger station.

Suddenly, Delgado ran toward a bulletin board. He'd spotted something, and Chloe hurried to follow. She caught up with him standing beneath a lost-dog flyer with Chloe's picture on it!

"Is that you?" Delgado asked in disbelief. In the photo her fur was blown dry, and her diamond collar was gleaming.

"I can't believe Rachel's looking for me," Chloe said with amazement. In a week of surprises, this was perhaps the biggest one of all.

Rachel was thanking the innkeeper for her hospitality and preparing to leave. But it was hard to speak over Rafa's constant whining. She wasn't sure what was up with him, although the innkeeper didn't seem to mind.

"We always kept a dog when my husband was alive," she said kindly, looking down at the small dog.

Rachel perked up. "He'd make a wonderful companion," she told the innkeeper. "You're perfect for each other."

"Just like you and your boyfriend," the innkeeper said with a wink.

Rachel's cheeks turned pink. "Oh, we're not together."

The innkeeper looked at her skeptically. "That's too bad," she said, as if she didn't believe it. Then she turned and scratched Rafa's head gently.

"You're in, amigo," said Papi to Rafa when he saw the kind look on the innkeeper's face. "Congratulations!"

Suddenly, Rafa had a new home. Just then, Sam walked over, snapping his cell phone shut. "That was Ramirez. They found Chloe! She's up at Basaseachi Park!"

CHAPTER FOURTEEN

Sam and Rachel drove quickly across the countryside to Basaseachi, the tires of their rental car squealing as they peeled into the parking lot. They were so focused on what awaited them, they failed to notice the white van on their tail the whole time. But Papi took note of it. He sat up and stuck his nose out the window. His nose twitched—a scent he knew was coming from that van.

"Claro!" he exclaimed, turning to Manuel and Chico on the seat beside him. "That van. My Chloe has been in there."

Once both vehicles had stopped, Papi watched as Rafferty and Vasquez left the van, and then he climbed out through the car's half-open window. He had to investigate while the people were gone.

"Right on, Mighty Dog," Manuel cheered. "Power to the Papi!"

"I thought we'd never get rid of him," he muttered to Chico as soon as Papi had left. He scurried over to Rachel's purse and jumped inside.

Meanwhile, Rachel and Sam walked up to the front desk of the ranger station. Delgado was tethered on a leash and sat quietly near the desk. "Hi," said Rachel. "We're here for my dog, Chloe?"

"Sure thing," the ranger at the desk said helpfully. "She's just out back." He called to another ranger who had escorted Chloe outside to take care of her business.

Behind the ranger station, Chloe was just inspecting a bush before stepping into the greenery. But Chloe hadn't noticed that she wasn't alone in the bushes. As she gave the spot one last sniff, she heard a low growl. *"Chi-chi-WOW-ha."* Chloe's heart skipped a beat. She hadn't been called that since she'd escaped the dogfights. . . .

Outside the bush, the ranger heard a short bark before the leash he held sagged to the ground. Stunned, he reeled it in . . . only to find that Chloe was gone!

He'd heard nothing, but the keen ears of Delgado and Papi had heard El Diablo's growl and Chloe's pitiful cry for help.

In a fury, Delgado broke free of his own leash and headed for where he'd last heard Chloe. "Kid! Kid!" he called. "Where are you?" But without his sense of smell, he had no clue how to look for his friend.

Back in the station, Sam looked around and realized that Papi was missing. "Where's Papi?" he asked. "Papi!" It didn't take him long to figure it out. "I bet he's gone after her," he said to Rachel.

They'd come to the park to find *one* dog, and now *three* were missing.

El Diablo charged through the jungle with Chloe hanging from his jaws. He finally stopped at a spot at the base of an ancient pyramid—the white van was there waiting for him. Rafferty and Vasquez emerged from the van, and El Diablo dropped a trembling Chloe at their feet.

Vasquez praised the Doberman. "Good work, El Diablo."

Then Vasquez fixed his cold gaze on Chloe. "You've been a lot of trouble. You better be worth it." To Rafferty, he added, "I need to call the owner. Put the dogs in the van and let's go. Better leave El Diablo up front with me. He can't have the Chihuahua until after I get my money."

Chloe thought sadly of how close she'd come to a reunion with Viv. Or even a reunion with Rachel. Her visit to Techichi seemed like a million years ago, and, right now, Chloe felt like anything but a warrior.

Rafferty threw open the back gate of the van and prepared to toss Chloe in. But in a flash, Papi burst from the hold, right into Rafferty's chest! Rafferty fell back, dropping Chloe to the ground.

Chloe stood there, blinking in disbelief. "Papi? What are you doing here?"

"Rescuing you!" yelled Papi. "Run!" The two Chihuahuas took off, ducking under and racing around debris on the jungle floor. A pyramid suddenly blocked their path, so they scurried up its stairs until they reached the very top. They could hear El Diablo smashing through the underbrush as he chased after them.

"We're trapped!" Chloe screamed. El Diablo was now bounding up the stairs of the pyramid, with Vasquez and Rafferty close behind.

Papi planted himself in front of Chloe. "I will protect you, *mi corazon*."

Chloe took one step backward and fell into a hole in the pyramid. In a heartbeat she managed to grab on to the ledge with her front paws.

"Hold on, Chloe!" Papi shouted.

But Chloe watched in horror as Rafferty appeared behind Papi and grabbed him!

And then Vasquez's arms snaked down for her. Chloe squeezed her eyes shut and let her paws go. Anything—absolutely anything— would be better than being in his clutches again. She allowed herself to drop into the void.

Delgado was turning around in circles in the ranger station's parking lot. He was angry and disappointed that he couldn't follow Chloe's scent, but then a movement caught his eye. It was Manuel and Chico, and they were running off with Chloe's collar!

"You two!" Delgado snarled. "What are you doing here?"

The cohorts stopped in their tracks. "It's not what you think, man!" Chico cried. "We're not stealing the collar. Okay, maybe we are, but—"

"Look, man," interrupted Manuel. "What my partner's trying to say is, if you hurry, you can pick up her scent using this." Wincing, he offered his prize possession up to Delgado.

But Delgado only looked back at him in despair. "I . . . can't," he said.

Manuel was shocked. "What? I make this noble gesture and you're not even gonna try?"

Delgado looked at the ground. Manuel's words had hit a nerve. He leaned down and sniffed the collar hesitantly, just in case, but he smelled nothing.

119

"What's the point of having that big thing on the end of your face, then?" the rat mocked.

Delgado growled and sniffed again with everything he had. Still, there was nothing.

"She needs you, man!" Chico shrieked.

Delgado's nostrils flared as he sniffed harder and harder, knowing Chico was right. He'd gotten Chloe this far, and without him she couldn't get much farther. He was all she had! He had to find her scent! Maybe if he just believed in himself . . . Delgado took deeper and deeper whiffs, refusing to give up. Suddenly, something changed. He could smell the collar. He could smell!

"He's got it!" Manuel cried, seeing the look on Delgado's face.

Without another word, Delgado yanked the collar away from the rat and ran for the ranger station. He bounded inside, skidding up next to Rachel and Sam. Detective Ramirez had joined them, and he and the rangers looked with interest at the German shepherd. Carefully, Delgado set the collar down on the floor in front of them.

"It's Chloe's collar," Rachel said.

Delgado barked twice, crisply, then raised his nose up in the air.

"He's found her scent," Detective Ramirez realized. He looked at Delgado and used a hand signal. When Delgado barked, Detective Ramirez broke into a grin. "This dog's been trained. He wants to lead us to the Chihuahua!"

CHAPTER FIFTEEN

Chloe awoke in total darkness. At first she was confused, but then the details trickled back one by one. El Diablo. Vasquez. Papi! And now she was trapped! She whimpered with fear.

With all the courage she could muster, Chloe stood up. She flinched as spiderwebs hit her face, then she dropped back to the floor, whining. Something scurried in the blackness, and she cringed and bumped against the wall in an effort to move away.

Then, with a rumble, streams of dirt began to rain down from above her. Chloe closed her eyes and curled up, frozen with terror.

And then it stopped.

Opening one eye, Chloe realized that the room had begun to glow with a dim light. She was in a chamber below a skylight. And in the shaft of light that fell from above was a statue . . . of Margarita! Maybe she was losing her mind, but Chloe was sure she could hear the warrior's voice calling, "*Adelita!*" She suddenly remembered Margarita telling her of the power and strength inside each Chihuahua.

As her eyes adjusted, Chloe discovered she was in a corridor with multiple tunnels branching out in all directions. Her tour through Aztec history came back to her, and she knew just what she was looking at.

"This is a Chihuahua tunnel," Chloe

said with new hope. Buoyed by the remote possibility that she could escape, Chloe chose a tunnel and headed out.

Delgado followed Chloe's scent through the jungle, while Rachel, Sam, Detective Ramirez, and the rangers tried to keep up. He burst into a clearing and spotted the pyramid with the empty white van parked outside. Thanks to his police-dog training, he assessed the situation quickly: everyone he was looking for was inside the pyramid. He just hoped he could shake off the terrible memories of the last time he'd helped a rescue mission.

The German shepherd stepped into a crumbling passageway, then stopped and stiffened. He gave a silent signal to Detective Ramirez, who held the others back. Just then, Rafferty rounded a corner and disappeared into the pyramid. Delgado had to stop him before he got any closer to Chloe!

* ★ ★

But while Delgado was still searching for Chloe, El Diablo had already sniffed her out. The Doberman stood near the entrance to a tunnel, while Vasquez consulted with Rafferty on a walkie-talkie. "I know you're here, *chica*," El Diablo growled softly, so only Chloe could hear.

He stuck his nose into the tunnel and snapped, "I can smell you!"

Behind him and out of sight, Chloe popped her head out of another tunnel and stuck her tongue out at El Diablo. For now, at least, her size was an advantage.

"No sign of the dog here," Vasquez said into the walkie-talkie as he watched the Doberman sniffing around the tunnel. On the other end of the line there was only static. "Rafferty?" Vasquez said. "Where are you?"

Chloe's ears pricked up when she heard the sounds of a scuffle coming over the transmission. Then came a shrill bark. She was sure the barking dog was Delgado. And if she knew Delgado, he had Rafferty under control.

Chloe waited until Vasquez moved away from her and then jumped out of her hiding spot. Vasquez was distracted by his walkie-talkie, so she looked around and spotted Papi in a cage near his feet. She silently pulled the cage's latch out with her teeth.

Papi whistled under his breath. "Whoa! Who have you been hanging around with?"

She shushed him and motioned for him to follow her into a tunnel.

Suddenly, Vasquez turned around. He started to say something, but then he stopped and stared at the empty cage that Papi had been in only moments before.

Chloe managed to reach the safety of a tunnel, but before Papi could follow her, El Diablo realized what was going on. Now the Doberman was blocking Papi's path. With a snarl, he charged Papi, but the Chihuahua darted out of the way easily.

"You're kinda clumsy for a fighter," Papi taunted. El Diablo growled as he stalked forward. When Papi dived in the opposite direction, he found Vasquez blocking the way!

"Get him, Diablo," Vasquez ordered.

Chloe watched from the tunnel. The scene unfolded as if it were in slow motion. With gleaming eyes, El Diablo closed in for the kill, while Papi shrank away. Suddenly, Vasquez appeared and reached out to grab Chloe. But she managed to slip away before he got a hold of her. She yipped in panic as she ran for her life.

Chloe's yip echoed through the pyramid, but then Chloe heard another sound. It was Margarita's voice again. "Find your bark, *Adelita*," said the voice. "Find your bark!"

Vasquez closed in on her just as El Diablo prepared for his final lunge at Papi. Then something inside Chloe snapped. She knew she didn't need Viv or Rachel. She didn't even need Delgado. She closed her eyes and cleared her throat. Then she opened her mouth and let loose a mighty bark!

El Diablo stopped midlunge, and Vasquez dropped his walkie-talkie.

Papi murmured, *"Dios mio!"* under his breath.

Even Chloe was shocked by the power of her voice. "I . . . barked," she said, as if the others could have missed it. "I barked!"

Locking her gaze on El Diablo and Vasquez, Chloe let loose a terrifying barrage of barks. The chamber and the stone of the pyramid amplified the sound until the noise was almost unbearable, but Chloe kept at it. El Diablo flinched with every bark, his senses reeling. Faint cracks of light began to appear at the edges of the tunnel, as if the sound were tearing the place apart. Rock fragments and dust flew every which way.

A chunk of stone missed Vasquez by a hair, and he backed against the wall. For a moment he felt around for the exit. When he found it, he ran as fast as he could and didn't look back.

His gun drawn, Vasquez stumbled in the dim light of the tunnel. A moment later he ran right into something—Delgado! The German shepherd knocked him down and kept on running toward Chloe and Papi. Vasquez was on the ground feeling for his gun when Detective Ramirez discovered him. In seconds, Detective Ramirez had Vasquez in handcuffs.

Chloe stopped her loud, unearthly barking just as Delgado burst into the crumbling chamber. Papi and El Diablo were there, too, recovering from the barrage of sound. El Diablo pounced at Delgado, but the German shepherd spun just in time to avoid being pinned. He turned and attacked with equal ferocity. El Diablo was shocked.

Delgado stumbled on some loose debris and fell against the wall.

Instantly, El Diablo was in his face, leering. "I see you're no quicker than last time," he said. Delgado came back at him, but El Diablo was unfazed. "It doesn't matter. You'll only fail again."

As El Diablo advanced on Delgado, Chloe leaped! With another ferocious bark, she landed on the Doberman's back. But El Diablo shook her off as if she were water. Chloe's body slammed into a wall and then crumpled to the floor, motionless.

"Chloe!" Delgado cried. He ran to his friend and looked down at her still form.

As Delgado's eyes welled up, El Diablo snorted scornfully. It was too much. Delgado came at El Diablo with his teeth bared and his claws flashing. Landing squarely on him with all his might, the two tumbled end over end. "Still think you're a police dog? You can barely smell. You're barely a dog at all!"

Delgado hurtled into El Diablo, in a move almost identical to the one El Diablo pulled on him those many years ago. In a second, El Diablo was on his back, pinned and vulnerable.

Delgado bared his teeth again. "I *can* smell: I can smell your fear." He had El Diablo just where he wanted him.

While Delgado faced off with El Diablo, Papi walked over to Chloe. *"Mi corazon?"* he whispered. Delgado glanced over at the love-struck Chihuahua and felt sorry for him. When he looked back, El Diablo was gone!

But the time for vengeance had passed. Delgado had made his point, and now he had a friend to help.

"Kid?" Delgado asked, gently laying his paw on Chloe's.

Just then, Detective Ramirez rushed in with Sam and Rachel. Sam reunited happily with Papi, but Rachel sobbed as she picked up Chloe's limp body.

As Rachel cried, light began to shine in

from all the tunnel entrances in the chamber. It shot into the room, illuminating the floor as hundreds of ghostly Chihuahuas ran out of the tunnels! They ran up the walls of the great chamber all the way to the top of the pyramid, taking their places alongside the painted images of their ancestors.

At the top of the chamber, hovering in the air, were the spirit forms of Monte and Margarita. They floated down to have a word with Chloe.

"It is not your time, little one," said Monte comfortingly.

"You still have much to do," Margarita reminded her.

Monte nodded to the other Chihuahuas and they released a tremendous bark. Rachel and Sam covered their ears, Delgado dropped to the ground, and Papi appeared almost electrified.

At the sound, Chloe turned her head ever so slightly. She opened her eyes and looked up at Rachel. "Rachel, you didn't leave me!" she rasped.

"Chloe!" Rachel cried.

"The name's *Adelita*," Chloe said with a smile, even though Rachel couldn't understand. "Tiny but mighty."

CHAPTER SIXTEEN

Detective Ramirez had a word with Rachel and Sam while Vasquez and Rafferty waited in the back of his car.

"Thanks for your help catching Vasquez," he said earnestly. "You know, Ms. Ashe, not a lot of people would have gone to so much trouble for a dog. Your aunt should be proud of you."

Rachel squirmed. "Unfortunately, she'll probably be angry. And I can't say I blame her."

Rachel was trying to decide what in the world she would say to Viv about this whole adventure, when Sam playfully punched her in the arm.

"If we hit the road, she doesn't necessarily have to know," he said.

Chloe, Papi, and Delgado were sitting next to the police car when they saw Sam and Rachel walking toward them. Chloe and Papi stood to leave. Chloe couldn't wait to get back to Beverly Hills. If only she knew how to thank Delgado for all he'd done! Suddenly, something occurred to her.

"You know, Vivian could still use a guard dog," she told him.

Delgado shook his head. "Someone has to go after El Diablo. Besides, *Princesa*, I think you can take care of things yourself now."

"I'll miss you," Chloe said, fighting back tears.

"This isn't good-bye," Delgado insisted.

"We'll see each other again someday." He took one last wistful glance at the police cars and officers, then resolutely strode away.

Rachel turned to look at Detective Ramirez. "Maybe you could use some extra help on the force?" she suggested with a glance at the departing German shepherd.

Detective Ramirez thought for a moment and then whistled at Delgado. "Where do you think you're going, Officer?"

Delgado turned around and saw Detective Ramirez extending a leash to him.

"You ready to go back on the job?" the detective asked, smiling.

Delgado barked in response and wagged his tail.

As Sam and Rachel pulled away in the rental car, Chloe and Papi stuck their heads out the window.

"*Adios*, kid," Delgado yelled at Chloe.

"*Muchas gracias*, Delgado," Chloe yelled back. Her Spanish accent was perfect.

Delgado was about to fade from view, but Chloe could still hear his parting words to her. "Thank you, Chloe. I've never had a friend like you!"

Sam, Rachel, and the dogs beat Vivian back to Beverly Hills that night without a second to spare. Sam parked his truck out in front of Viv's mansion while Rachel scrambled inside, holding a filthy Chloe. It was bath time!

"Hurry!" Sam urged her. "She'll be here really soon!"

Minutes later, Viv's limousine pulled up in front of Sam and Papi. "Sam!" Viv gushed, kissing him on both cheeks. "I didn't expect to see you. It's good to be home. I can't wait to see Chloe!"

"Actually, Vivian," said Sam, doing his best to stall her, "there's something I need to show you in the garden."

But Vivian wasn't interested. "Whatever it is, Sam, we can go over it tomorrow. Now get some rest. You look exhausted. You've been working too hard!" Before Sam could stop her, Viv headed inside.

Vivian entered the front hall just as a soaking wet Rachel was coming down the stairs. "Rachel!" exclaimed her aunt. "Why are you wet?"

"I . . . uh, was in the bath," Rachel said uncomfortably. She wrapped her arms around Viv and added, "Welcome home!"

Sam and Papi entered the room, and Viv looked around expectantly. "Where's Chloe? She usually greets me."

Before anyone could answer, Chloe descended the stairs like a princess. Her diamond collar was flashing, and every strand of fur was in place. She looked as if she'd never left the mansion and beamed as Vivian scooped her up.

"There's my precious Chloe." Viv looked at Rachel. "Thank you for taking such good care of her!" She nuzzled Chloe and breathed deeply before making a face. "What's that smell?"

Rachel felt her heart skip a beat.

"Is that a new shampoo? It's so . . . earthy and urban and . . . I love it!"

"I can't do this," Rachel blurted out. Sam looked at her and nodded in understanding. "The truth is, I took Chloe to Mexico and she got stolen and thrown into the dog-fights," she admitted. "She spent the last week roaming Mexico with an ex–police dog, and these really bad men were after her!" Rachel paused for breath before finishing. "I know you'll never trust me again. I'm really sorry, Aunt Viv."

While Viv took it all in, Sam looked proudly at Rachel. "What Rachel left out, Vivian, is that she never gave up searching for Chloe, and, because of that, we got her back."

Viv sighed and threw up her hands. "I guess it's been quite a week." She gave Rachel a stern look. "I can't say I'm pleased you took Chloe to Mexico, but it's very responsible of you to have told me the truth when you could have gotten away with it."

Rachel was relieved. "I promise I'll never do anything like that again," she told her aunt. Then she gave Chloe an affectionate scratch, and Chloe licked her in return.

Later that night, Chloe and Papi sat quietly together under the stars on Viv's patio. Chloe had some apologies of her own to make. "After the way I treated you," she said, "I can't believe you came after me!"

"How could I not?" Papi asked.

He had always been open with Chloe about his feelings, but now it was Chloe's turn to be open about hers. *"Papi, tu eres mi corazon,"* she whispered.

"I think I'm going to cry!" Papi said, smiling through his tears.

The two Chihuahuas snuggled closer and lay back to enjoy a new beginning, together.

Get More of Your Favorite Pop Star!

Bonus:
8 postcards to send to friends!

Includes 12 posters of the show's stars!

Collect all the stories about Hannah Montana!

DISNEY PRESS
AN IMPRINT OF DISNEY BOOK GROUP

www.disneybooks.com

Available wherever books are sold